The Bunny Who Found Easter

To Steve, who gave me the idea
—C.Z.

To Crumb, who arrived with the rabbits
—H.C.

The
Bunny
Who Found
Easter

CHARLOTTE ZOLOTOW
ILLUSTRATED BY HELEN CRAIG

HOUGHTON MIFFLIN HARCOURT
Boston New York

One day a little bunny woke up from
a long nap alone under a tall elm tree.
He heard the silence of the woods
around him and wanted other rabbits
like himself for company.

"Can you tell me where I will find other rabbits?" he asked a sleepy old owl in the elm tree.

"Other rabbits?" said the owl. "Why, there are always rabbits at Easter."

"Where is Easter?" asked the little bunny eagerly.

But the old owl had dozed off to sleep again in the bright sun. "It must be some place to the East," thought the bunny and he set off searching.

It was a hot summer day. The leaves in the trees stood as still as a painting against the blue sky. The bunny found a pool of water, and down in the water silvery trout flashed by. But there were no bunnies about.

"Then this can't be Easter," he thought, and went on his way.

He came to a field full of daisies.
There was a hot summer daisy smell
over the field and the bunny's nose
twinkled. A big slow bumblebee hummed
by. But in all that whiteness of daisies
there was no whiteness of bunnies like
himself.

"This isn't Easter," the bunny said,
and he went on.

Once he was caught in a summer storm. The sky looked like night. Suddenly a streak of lightning, the color of the stars, forked through the sky. Great rumblings rolled from one end of the world to the other. The rain came down so fast that the bunny could hardly see the mountain laurel just ahead.

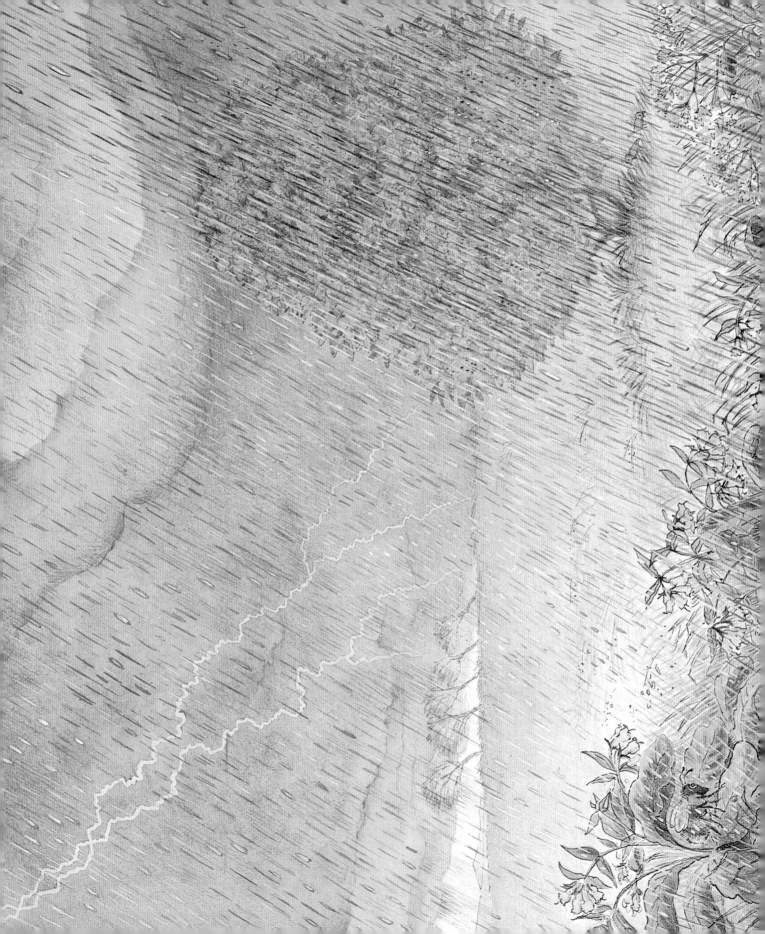

Slowly the rumbling rolled by.
Slowly the sky brightened.
Slowly the rain stopped.

He could see the
mountain laurel with
the wet shining leaves,
each flower cup filled
with one sparkling
drop of rain.

But he couldn't see any other bunnies shaking the rain off their wet white fur.

"Not Easter," he said sadly, and hurried on his way.

Summer was nearly over. The leaves on the forest trees began to turn, brown and gold and red.

Dead leaves crackled under the soft rabbit hops of the little bunny who was looking for Easter.

He stopped under a tree to rest and a round shiny red apple fell down and startled him.

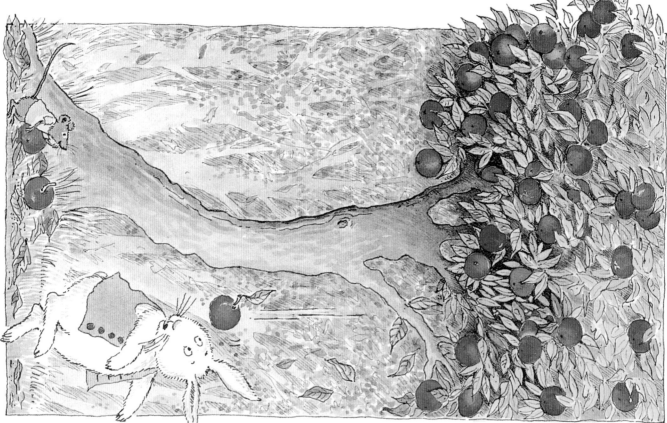

It smelled of autumn and crispness.
He took a bite with his two front sharp teeth.

When he had crunched the apple to its seeds, he looked around and sighed.

There wasn't another bunny to be seen.

One day it began to snow. Soft white flakes drifted down from the sky, and the air was sharp and cold and still. When he hopped through the white drifts he left little dark footprints in the snow. But no matter which way he hopped, his footprints never crossed other bunny footprints. The little bunny was alone in a world without rabbits.

There were birds, little
black sparrows like ink
drops in the snow.

Brown squirrels
leaped about in the bare
branches of the trees.

But there wasn't another long-eared, pink nosed, white furry rabbit like himself to be seen.

"This can't be Easter yet," he thought, and his loneliness grew inside of him.

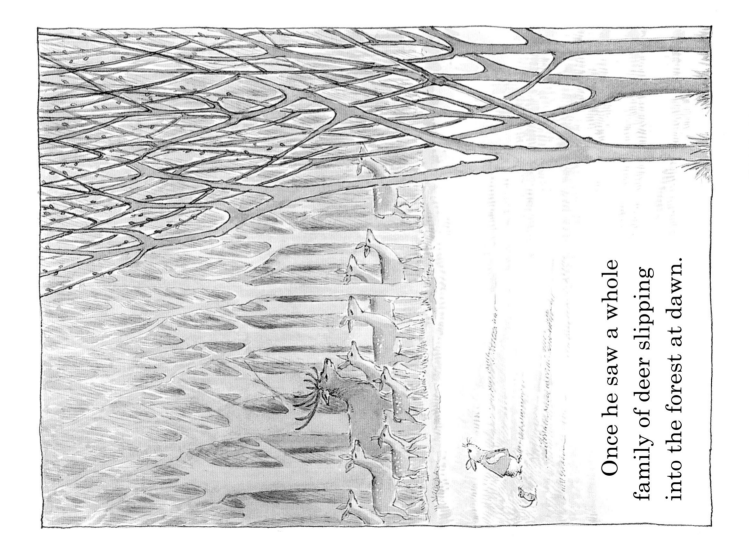

Once he saw a whole family of deer slipping into the forest at dawn.

That night the bunny curled
up in a hollow tree to keep
himself warm out of the wind
and sharp air.

When he woke up the next
morning there was something
different.

It smelled . . . he quivered
his nose and smelled hard . . .
it smelled of greenness and
warm soft sunlight.

The little bunny felt sure he
would come to Easter soon.

In the forest the black twigs had little tight curled green buds. The birds were singing high up in the trees as the bunny hopped ahead looking for Easter.

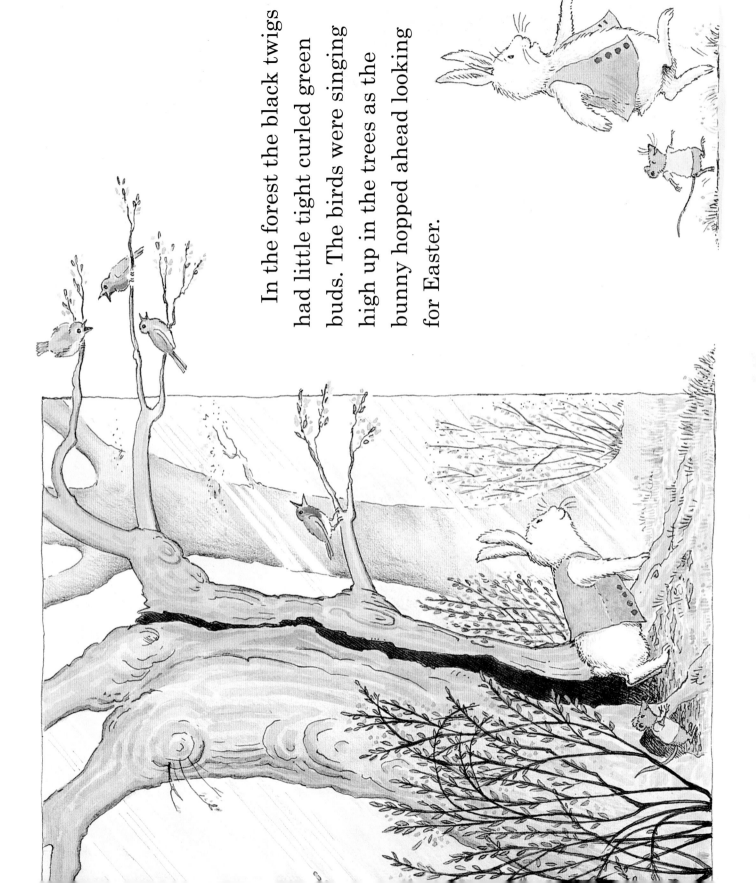

Suddenly he saw something in the muddy earth that made him stand perfectly still with excitement. Crossing in front of him, and going into the woods where he had never been, were little rabbit paw prints on the ground!

He followed the paw prints very carefully down a hidden path. There, in a clearing, he saw someone small and furry resting on a mossy bank.

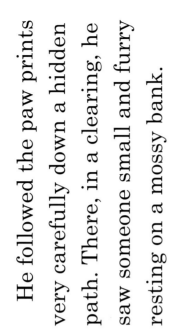

It was another bunny!
She had brown fur.
She had long ears like
himself, and eager
bright eyes, like himself.

The little bunny
was so happy to find
her, he completely
forgot about Easter.

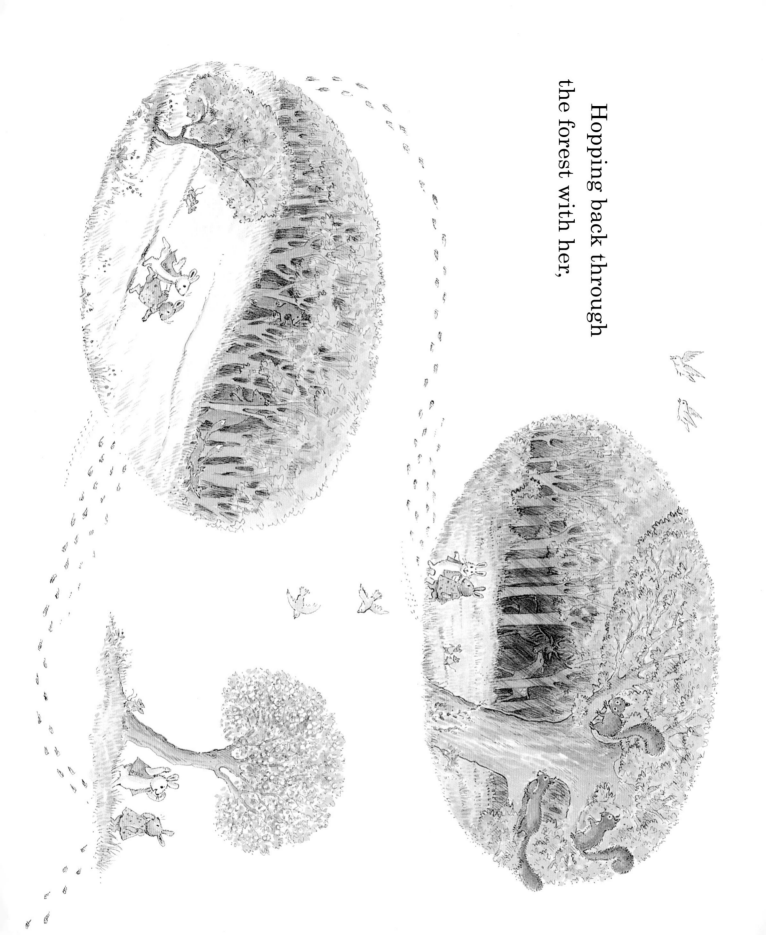

Hopping back through
the forest with her,

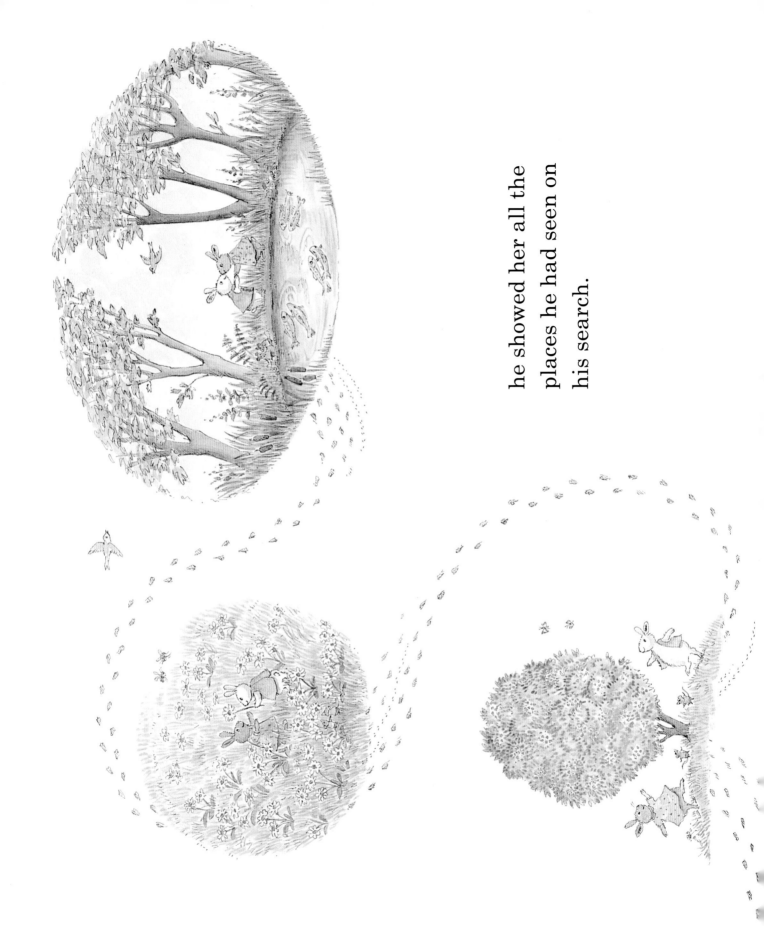

he showed her all the places he had seen on his search.

At last they came to the tall elm tree where he had first awakened to find himself alone. But now his loneliness was gone. The two bunnies were very happy together.

Soon they had a whole family of little rabbits, tiny, soft sleepy things with long sweet ears and small wet noses. The bunny's heart throbbed with happiness at this wonderful earthsmelling sunlit bunny-filled world.

"Aha!" said the old owl when he saw the bunny's family, "didn't I tell you so? At Eastertime there are always rabbits."

The bunny felt his little bunnies around him and the earth blooming beyond them, and all things growing. And he understood at last that Easter was not a *place* after all, but a *time* when everything lovely begins once again.